# Frank Rodgers

# Millie's Letter

SIMON & SCHUSTER
YOUNG BOOKS

Millie's dad was a sailor on a big ship and sometimes she didn't see him for ages and ages.

So Millie wrote a letter to her dad and posted it herself. Her birthday was in a few days and she wanted to make sure her dad would be there.

But as her birthday got nearer she thought,
"What if Dad doesn't get my letter?"

What if it gets stolen by Neptune, the King of the sea?

What if a giant sea-serpent eats it for breakfast?

What if the captain of Dad's ship is a pirate and chops my letter into little pieces with his cutlass?"

The night before Millie's birthday she could hardly sleep. As the moon shone into her bedroom she opened her eyes and saw a strange thing.

A small white shape floated through the open window and landed on the floor. Millie stared. It looked like her letter! What was it doing here?

She got out of bed to have a closer look. But the letter had grown to the size of her bedside rug and Millie found she was standing in the middle of it.

Suddenly the letter gave a little shiver and lifted off the ground. Millie sat down with a bump. The letter, with Millie aboard, sailed right out of the window and up into the sky.

"What if I fall off?" thought Millie.
But she didn't. The letter carried her like a great
bird high above the land and out over the sea.

On and on flew Millie on her letter.

Far below she saw a ship.
Down swooped Millie's letter.

The sailors were startled when Millie landed on the deck. "Jumping jellyfish!" they cried.

But it was Millie's dad's ship and he
ran up and gave her a huge hug.
"It's a special delivery!" he laughed.

"What's going on?" roared the captain grumpily.
But when he found out it was Millie paying a visit he smiled.
"Ship's cook!" he bellowed. "Prepare a feast!"

Everyone had a wonderful time. Dolphins and flying-fish played around the ship and King Neptune sang jolly sea-songs.

When the sea-serpent joined in everyone had to put their
hands over their ears because the noise was so awful.
"Time for games!" said the captain.

They played hide and seek all over the ship

and danced the hornpipe.

Dad gave Millie a birthday present.
"You mustn't open it until tomorrow," he said.

Millie laughed in delight but just as she took the present
the letter suddenly lifted her into the air again.
"Dad!" shouted Millie.

Millie's dad and the sailors jumped to catch hold of the
letter but it flew up and away out of their reach.
They waved after it sadly. "Goodbye, Millie!" they cried.
"We hope you have a lovely birthday!"

Millie soared high among the clouds
on the long journey home.
It was so long that Millie fell asleep.

She woke in her own bed to find it was morning.
On her bedside table was a package.
It was her birthday present from Dad.

She unwrapped the paper and found
a beautiful brass telescope inside.

"What if . . . ?" Millie thought, and rushe[d]
to the window. She looked north an[d]
she looked south. Suddenly she laughe[d].
"Mum!" she called. "Come and see[!]

Mum looked through the telescope
and laughed too.

This is what they saw.
Millie's dad was coming home for her birthday after all. And in his hand he held Millie's letter.

First published in Great Britain in 1993
by Simon & Schuster Young Books
Campus 400
Maylands Avenue
Hemel Hempstead
Herts HP2 7EZ

Typeset in 16pt Bembo Educational by Goodfellow & Egan Ltd, Cambridge
Printed and bound in Belgium by Proost International Book Productions

British Library Cataloguing in Publication Data available

ISBN: 0 7500 1273 0
ISBN: 0 7500 1274 9 (pbk)